It had been an umbrella day after all.

When she opened them again, the squirrel, frog and butterfly were gone.

Missy shook out the tattered umbrella and snapped it shut.

And it did.

The boat popped out of the tunnel of water. The waves ran back, the winds calmed, the sun beamed down, and the umbrella glided across the water and nudged against the shore.

Missy closed her eyes and sighed.

Then suddenly the whirlpool rolled over on its side and became a tunnel of water. Swish! They turned over and over as they rushed toward the tunnel—only water and darkness all around. So she grabbed the mast and shook it. "Stop!" she commanded.

And the pond turned into a lake, and the lake turned into an ocean.

They rushed toward open water. The boat bobbed and dipped. The six tumbled together—butterfly, frog, squirrel, dog, kitten and Missy.

"This is too much!" Missy shouted out loud. But even as she said it, she saw a whirlpool just ahead. The boat spun faster and faster.

The umbrella changed into a boat, a small boat, but there was plenty of room for three. So they climbed in and sailed away.

The stream grew into a pond. As they floated gently along, a butterfly landed on the tip of Missy's nose. The water began to get rougher. A frog jumped in. He didn't take up much room. The waves got a little higher. Down from the branches leaped a squirrel. Missy let it stay too.

But when a huge elephant decided to come too close, Missy felt uneasy. So she peeked out from under the edge of the tent.

It had stopped raining. But the brook was rising and had circled their hill.

All around them the water rose higher. Their hill was shrinking. Missy grabbed the handle and ordered, "Be a boat."

And the toadstool ballooned into a huge wild animal tent. Luckily, Missy was a good trainer and tamed the lion with no trouble at all. She even had time to dance with the bear. She made the tigers roll over and beg for leftover raspberry tarts.

When they rested, Missy looked at the toadstool. An adventure might be nice.

"Be a wild animal tent, then," she said.

And it was.

A table even sprouted out of the ground, all set with daisy cups and dishes. So Missy and her dog and kitten sat down and ate raspberry tarts, drank mint tea, and sang a song in pops to match the raindrops falling on the toadstool.

And just in time.

But it felt stuffy and crowded under that umbrella. If this were only a toadstool over their heads, she could be an elf and have a tea-break with plenty of room. So she said to the umbrella, "Be a toadstool."

She tugged at the clasp with her fingers. She shoved with her hands to get it open. Finally she pushed the bent metal ribs with her feet until they clicked into place.

Missy saw some daisies across the brook. She jumped across the water and sat down to make a chain of the daisies.

Suddenly two or three big, fat drops of rain fell on her head. She needed that umbrella up!

and then rolled down again.

Still, she could rescue her kitten from the bushes with the silly, bent tip. And she could block her dog's path so he couldn't catch the squirrel he was chasing. And she could use the umbrella as a wobbly cane when she climbed a hill

Missy frowned as she stomped along. Her mother had told her it was an umbrella day. But Missy was sure it wouldn't rain. She couldn't even find her own umbrella, only this big, old, dusty one from the back of the closet.

To my mother, Grace, my sisters Betty and
Flora Ann, and to Patti, who remembered

N.E.C.

For Duffy

M.B.M.

Text copyright © 1989 by Nancy Evans Cooney
Illustrations copyright © 1989 by Melissa Bay Mathis
All rights reserved. This book, or parts thereof,
may not be reproduced in any form
without permission in writing from the publisher.
A PaperStar Book, published in 1997 by
The Putnam & Grosset Group,
200 Madison Avenue, New York, NY 10016.
PaperStar Books and the PaperStar logo
are trademarks of The Putnam Berkley Group, Inc.
Originally published in 1989 by Philomel Books.
Printed simultaneously in Canada.
Printed in the United States of America.
Library of Congress Cataloging-in-Publication Data
Cooney, Nancy Evans.
The umbrella day / Nancy Cooney;
illustrated by Melissa Bay Mathis. p. cm.
Summary: Missy unwillingly carries her umbrella,
having been assured by her mother that it is an umbrella day;
and sure enough, unbelievable adventures happen,
making her glad and grateful for that accessory.
[1. Umbrellas and parasols—Fiction.]
I. Mathis, Melissa, ill. II. Title.
PZ7.C7843Um 1988 [E]—dc19 87-16730 CIP AC
ISBN 0-698-11562-7

1 3 5 7 9 10 8 6 4 2

BE CKY

The Umbrella Day

by Nancy Evans Cooney

illustrations by

Melissa Bay Mathis

PaperStar

The Putnam & Grosset Group

The
Umbrella Day